Pass

PUFFIN BOOKS
UK | USA | Canada | Ireland | Australia | India | New Zealand | South Africa
Puffin Books is part of the Penguin Random House group of companies
whose addresses can be found at global.penguinrandomhouse.com.
puffinbooks.com
First published 2016
001
Text and illustrations copyright © Sophy Henn, 2016
The moral right of the author/illustrator has been asserted
A CIP catalogue record for this book is available from the British Library
Printed in China
Hardback ISBN: 978–0–723–29985–1
Paperback ISBN: 978–0–723–29986–8

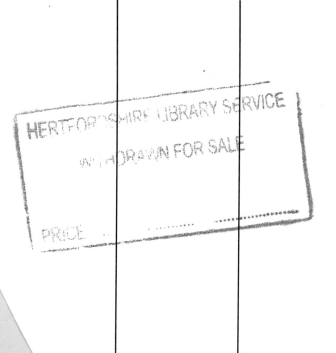

It On

by

Sophy Henn

PUFFIN

When
YOU
see
something
TERRIFIC...

. . . smile a smile
    and pass it on.

If you chance upon a chuckle,

hee hee hee
and pass it on.

If something happens
that's amazing,
whoop it up
and pass it on.

Should you spot
a thing of wonder,

jump for joy
and pass it on.

With all the smiles you have made
and the joy you've spread about,
you'll find the world's
a little nicer . . .

and those smiles
a little brighter.

Sometimes the fun and glee
aren't in their usual place.
But search around,
there's always some . . .

a hum, a hug, a happy face.

So when the sky
is grey and rainy,
you'll know just what to do . . .

grab your wellies and your mac,

splash a smile and pass it on.

If you feel a little lonely,
don't let that worry you.
Just branch out,
see who's there,

find some fun

and pass it on.

And when you least expect it,
like a bolt out of the blue,
a smile or a chuckle
will be passed . . .

right back to **you**.

Enjoy that **happy** moment,
let that feeling fill you up!

Then . . .

Have a ball,
    raise the roof,
  kick your heels
        and . . .

pass
it
on!

Huge thanks to two things of wonder, Alice and Goldy

Happy Hats